Hello!

My name is Hans. Welcome to my story.

You might know me from some of your favorite stories: "The Little Mermaid," "The Princess and the Pea," or "The Ugly Duckling."

My full name is Hans Christian. But you can call me H.C. That's what my friends call me. Plus, if we shorten my name to "H.C.," we'll have more room to write our adventure.

I am a teller of stories, specifically of fairy tales. And have I got a story for you.

I was born in Odense, Denmark, on April 2, 1805. The city is southwest of Denmark's capital, Copenhagen.

When I was young, I received a magic hat. When I put my hat on my head, I am transported to marvelous places with marvelous people. Well, for the most part. There have been some not-so-marvelous people.

But every story needs a villain.

I invite you to join me on my adventures.

So grab a hat—a baseball cap, a cowboy hat, one of those hats with a tiny propeller on top! If you don't have a hat, just use your imagination. You'll be using it a lot.

P.S. If you're wondering what part of this adventure comes from my imagination and what part comes from the real world, read "The H.C. Chronicles" at the back.

GRAB YOUR HAT AND GET READY FOR AN ADVENTURE!

HA,HA!
Did we scare you?

That was some entrance!

You know me, Poe.

Hi, Agatha.

Dame Agatha, to you!

Sorry, H.C., but I couldn't leave my latest scribblings at home. I hope you don't mind.

No, not at all!

Good evening, Dr. Seuss!

Good, we're all here now...

The story that you're about to hear isn't for the faint of heart. It's the true story of a ghost named Urbanus, a monk to be exact...

5

Where am I?
This doesn't look
like my house.

No matter! A person in His Majesty's
uniform isn't afraid of a challenge.
I'll find the way home.

BWAAA

Hahaha!!!

Quack!!! Quack!!!

Wait! What's happening? Where did you ducks go?

What's the matter with you?

Get back to work!

Where did you get that hat?

A talking pig? No way!

Can... can you talk, pig?

?

WAAAA!

Give me that hat! You don't know what power it holds!

AAAAAAA

Quack!!!

???

Hi!

Hi...
huh...
what?

How strange.
It's like the last
time my hat
acted out.

???

...

Who's there?

Is my grandfather home?

Hi, Hans! Yes, come in.

Young Hans! You're just in time for tea.

There's someone here who'd like to speak with you.

Sit down! And who would that be?

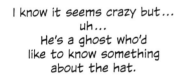

I know it seems crazy but... uh... He's a ghost who'd like to know something about the hat.

Ha, ha, ha! That's a good one, Hans. Do you want sugar in your tea?

But it's true! You have to listen to me!

I told my grandfather everything that had happened: that the hat didn't work, that I'd met a ghost monk, and that he had to speak with him because the hat could kill me!

...so you see, he has to talk to you!

15

Listen, Hans. It's just your imagination playing tricks on you. If you're not careful, people will think you're as crazy as I am!

He doesn't believe a word I'm saying!

??

Hmm, let's try something else. Repeat what I say.

Start with bla bla bla bla bla bla bla bla bla bla bla...

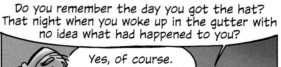

Do you remember the day you got the hat? That night when you woke up in the gutter with no idea what had happened to you?

Yes, of course. I told you about it.

Do you remember when you put on the hat for the first time? You were with your favorite things?

You were with your friends...

... you couldn't take any more...

... and when you said "enough," the food turned into dirt...

... your drink into blood and your friends into monsters...

But...

I never told you that... I had forgotten it myself. How...?

The ghost created the hat, so he can see everything the hat has experienced. Do you believe me now?

What does he want from me?

...........!!!
.........!!!

He wants to know if you touched the man who gave you the hat.

Yes, I shook his hand. I thought it was the gentlemanly thing to do. What about it??

Finally! After all these years, I'll finally be able to escape this curse!

Uh... wait... what curse? You didn't say anything about a curse. You were talking about a bird...

That's right, the bird. I'll tell you the rest of the story...

I followed the sparrow deep into the forest, until...

What is he saying?

I'll tell you as soon as he finishes.

Hello. Who... who are you?

Hello, Urbanus. I was waiting for you.

How do you know my name?

I'm here to help you. I heard your wishes.

I gave him the only things I had to my name, but I didn't realize that until it was too late. You may have heard people say that love is blind. Don't doubt it for a second!

Why did he need all that?

To make the hat. For it to work, he needed these three things from a holy man. He used my soul. Since then, I've been carrying this curse...

But enough is enough. I can finally end this madness!

Hans, are you ready to meet him?

Meet him? What do you mean?

There's a small chance that your grandfather can lead me to him. What are we waiting for???

Let's go!!!

There, that's all he said. What do you think? Are you coming with us?

Suuure... why not... a little fresh air will do me good, especially after such an incredible story...

Your grandfather is the only living person I've met who's touched him... and that contact could lead us to his world.

Excuse me, H.C., but who was this person you were going after?

The only person I still fear. A horrible creature!

I would have never followed the monk, if I'd known how the story would end.

That's for sure.

I always fear the end of stories... that's when the whodunit is revealed!

I don't need to finish your novel *Death on the Nile*... I know who did it!

Really?

Yes... I just watched the movie!

DEATH ON THE NILE

You see, my hat was neither the first nor last of its kind. The monk explained to me what they'd been created for...

Enough! If I don't leave immediately, I'll drop dead right here! We must turn back, Hans.

...

He doesn't want to go on. He'll hurt himself if he keeps this up!

Aaahh!!!

Then it's here.

25

Hans, tell your grandfather to wait for us at the edge of the woods.

???

No need to tell me twice!

Out of my way!!

¡¡HA!

I thought he couldn't hear you?

???

But how...?

I don't know. But your grandfather is safe now.

26

Well, well... nothing has changed. What do you think?

Ahhhhhhh!

You're absolutely right, he lays it on a bit thick. He's very theatrical.

Apparently he had a difficult childhood. **Come on!**

Halt! Who goes there?

This way... getting warmer... warmer... you're burning HOT!

We're here to speak to him...

One moment, your names?

Urbanus.

And you, young one?

Hans Christian Andersen...

Who are these people?

I'm not sure, boss. Only one of the names is on the list.

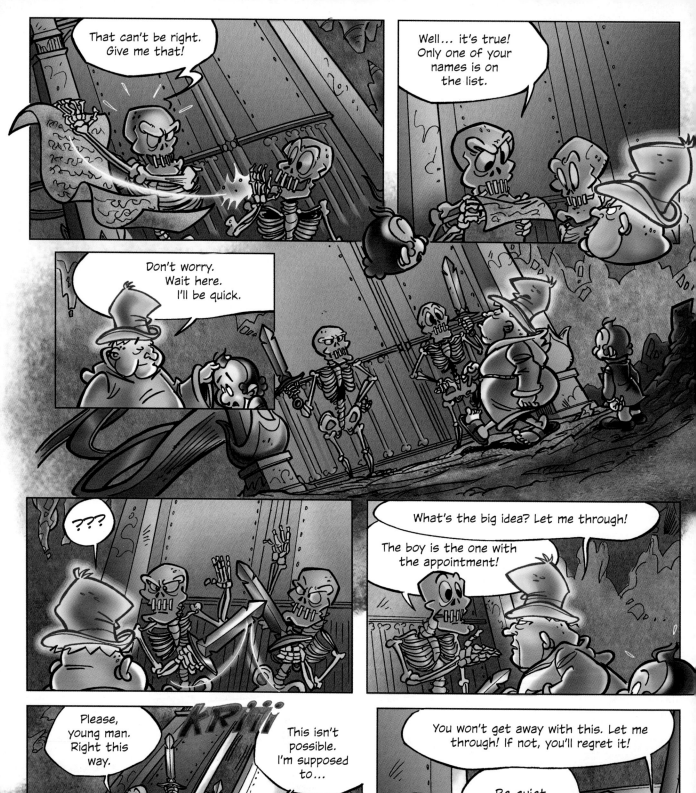

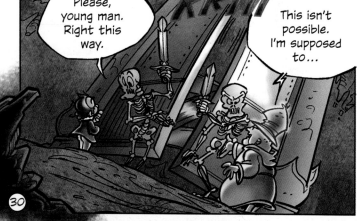

Good evening, gentlemen. Let's start this interview...

What's going on here?

Urbanus?

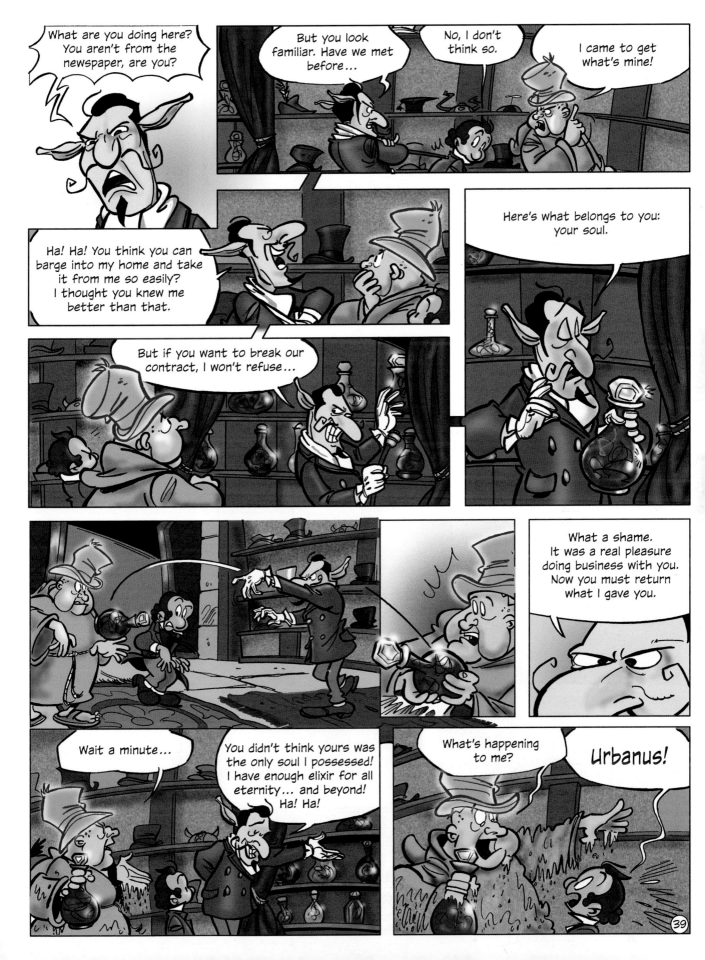

Love is fickle, isn't it?

PLOP!

Oh yes, one last thing...

That... that burns!

That should be enough to make sure you never come back here. I bid you farewell, young Andersen!

HAHAHA!!

...Urbanus, I have to...

42

Ha! Ha! Isn't it great? I'm finally in control...

I can touch things! I can feel things!

How'd we get out?

We were thrown out. Wear the hat as much as you like. It doesn't work.

What??? Impossible!

No, no! Why?

Hans, the hat contained Urbanus's soul.

Yes, I know. And now he's got it back.

I'm glad you got your soul back, but I'll never get back my fantastic imagination...

Hans, your imagination has nothing to do with that hat. It's inside you, and nothing can make it disappear!

You know, this is probably for the best. Who knows what might have happened with that cursed hat.

I'm never coming back here again. I was so scared!

I'm afraid you're marked for life, Hans.

Now, I want to hear every detail of your journey.

45

THE H.C. CHRONICLES

When Urbanus told me that I could no longer use my hat, I was devastated. I feared I would never see my mermaids and soldiers and dancers again.

But then he told me that my imagination had nothing to do with my hat. He assured me that nothing can make my imagination disappear, not even that evil man we met in that evil place.

My imagination and creativity persisted. Although the hat made a great accessory. After all, it was unique and, well, magical.

I did not imagine all of the people or places in this book.

Read on to see who's who and what's what. You will also read some of my fairy tales. And you won't even have to put on a hat!

Readers, if I've learned anything from this adventure, it's that we all have a creative spirit inside of us. Be sure to explore it!

WHO'S WHO

Did you recognize any of my ghostly companions? I hope those in that old-timey car remembered to boo-ckle their seatbelts.

EDGAR ALLAN POE

You might have recognized my friend Edgar Allan Poe (1809-1849) by his iconic mustache. He was an American poet, short-story writer, and literary critic. He is very famous for a poem called "The Raven."

SOREN KIERKEGAARD

My fellow countryman Soren Kierkegaard (1813-1855) was a philosopher and religious thinker. He is considered a founder of existentialism. People who believe in this theory are called *existentialists.* They emphasize freedom and choice.

DANNY KAYE

Danny Kaye (1913-1987) was a comedian, singer, and actor. He played me in the 1952 movie about my life. He was known for his lively pantomimes. To *pantomime* means to act without words. You might be familiar with—or have tried to run away from—a person dressed in black-and-white stripes who pretends to be trapped in a box. That is a pantomime.

DR. SEUSS

Dr. Seuss (1904-1991) was a master of nonsense. While he had a "Dr." at the beginning of his name, he was not like any doctor you have ever known. He studied humorous drawings rather than humerus bones. Dr. Seuss's real name was Theodor Seuss Geisel. You might know some his books: *The Cat in the Hat, The Lorax,* and *Horton Hears a Who!*

VICTOR HUGO

Do you know the hunchback of Notre-Dame? Well, not personally. But you might know him from a movie or a book. The French writer Victor Hugo (1802-1885) created that character, along with many others. He is also famous for writing *Les Misérables*. Victor was a good friend of mine, in real life, as well as in the afterlife!

AGATHA CHRISTIE

Agatha Christie (1890-1976) was an English writer of detective stories. She was known for her clever plots. She was the best detective writer the world had ever seen. Sorry, Sir Arthur Conan Doyle—maybe his ghost will haunt me in the next book. I have several recurring characters in my stories. So did Agatha Christie. In *The Mysterious Affair at Styles*, Christie introduced Hercule Poirot, a Belgian private investigator. He appears in many of Christie's novels, including *The Murder of Roger Ackroyd*, *Murder on the Orient Express*, and *Death on the Nile*.

MARVELOUS MONUMENTS

There are many statues of me all around Denmark. I particularly like the statue next to Copenhagen City Hall. I have a book and a cane. I look into the distance as if to think, "What will I dream up next?" As happens with beloved public monuments, I am a bit discolored. Many people have touched my legs. My thighs are a beautiful copper color. Many children—and probably some adults—have climbed on my lap as if to listen to one of my many fairy tales.

I don't want to see THAT statue. I want to see the statue of H.C. Andersen!

One statue is in Chicago, Illinois, in the United States. I sit by the Lincoln Park Zoo—what a lovely place to be! People raised money to fund the statue. Kids were among my most gracious benefactors. They even donated a bit of their allowance to the campaign. I sit with a book, and a swan rests at my feet. The swan references one of my most famous tales, "The Ugly Duckling."

I am one of the many intriguing statues in Bratislava, Slovakia. I stand and look downward, while several of my characters surround me. My fingers are unlike the rest of my body. They are copper. It is supposedly good luck to touch them—people must have collected a lot of luck! Other interesting statues in Bratislava include a paparazzi and a man climbing up from the ground.

H.C. ANDERSEN BALLETS

Before becoming a writer of fairy tales, I pursued some other careers. I wanted to be a singer, an actor, and—my favorite—a dancer. Although I did not succeed in the ballet world, my stories did. Several choreographers have created ballets inspired by my stories, particularly "The Steadfast Tin Soldier." The dance tells the story of a paper doll ballerina and a toy soldier who is madly in love with her.

One of my closest friends was the Danish dancer and choreographer August Bournonville (1805-1879). He and I loved to travel. In fact, many of his travels inspired his ballets. He would incorporate dances from around the world into his works. In the late 1800's, August choreographed *The Steadfast Tin Soldier.* It was wonderful. I loved seeing my characters dance before me. I've thought about including August in my adventures, but I think he and I would get distracted talking about ballet.

August Bournonville

In 1975, the celebrated choreographer George Balanchine presented his version of *The Steadfast Tin Soldier.* Two people perform the ballet. That is called a *pas de deux.*

George Balanchine

The picture above is from the New York City Ballet's The Snow Queen.

My story "The Snow Queen" inspired Disney's Frozen. Here, a skater performs in Disney On Ice. There are several key elements of ice dancing: grace, skill, and expression. Those elements are also present in ballet.

MY PAPER CUTOUTS

Paper cutouts go especially well with fairy tales. As I told stories, I would fold and cut paper into elaborate—and sometimes not—figures and scenes. My fairy tales were unlike any at the time. And so were my paper cutouts.

In Europe in the 1800's, a type of paper cutout called a silhouette was very popular. A silhouette is the outline of someone, often in *profile* (from the side). Silhouettes consist of a dark figure on a light background. But I usually cut from white paper. And as a very special treat I cut colored paper. I also cut up concert programs, newspapers, old letters—even the leaves of a rubber tree.

Here is a collection of some of my paper cutouts. As you can see, I signed most of them. Be sure to practice your signature—it might be valuable one day.

I especially liked to cut a figure called a Pierrot, or a theater clown. The clown held a tray on its head. Many people have speculated what this character means. Some say that it represents someone selling figurines from their head. Others say the images represent important places in my life. One building resembles my birthplace. The windmill is much like the windmills in Denmark. And the swan represents me. My fairy tale "The Ugly Duckling" is autobiographical. It is a story of transformation.

Here is a display of paper cutouts at my museum in Copenhagen, Denmark.

THE UGLY DUCKLING

Once upon a time, an impatient mama duck waited for her eggs to hatch. One day, she heard a "Peep! Peep!" All but one egg hatched. While she waited, the mama duck marveled at her perfect ducklings. "Surely the last duckling will be as perfect as the others."

One day, the final egg cracked. The mama duck yelped, "What a creature! He is so big and ugly!" The other animals agreed.

But he performed all of his duckling duties well. The mama duck praised his good character and swimming skills. But the little duckling was bitten and pushed and ridiculed. Soon, the mama duck wished he would leave their pond. So the duckling decided to run away.

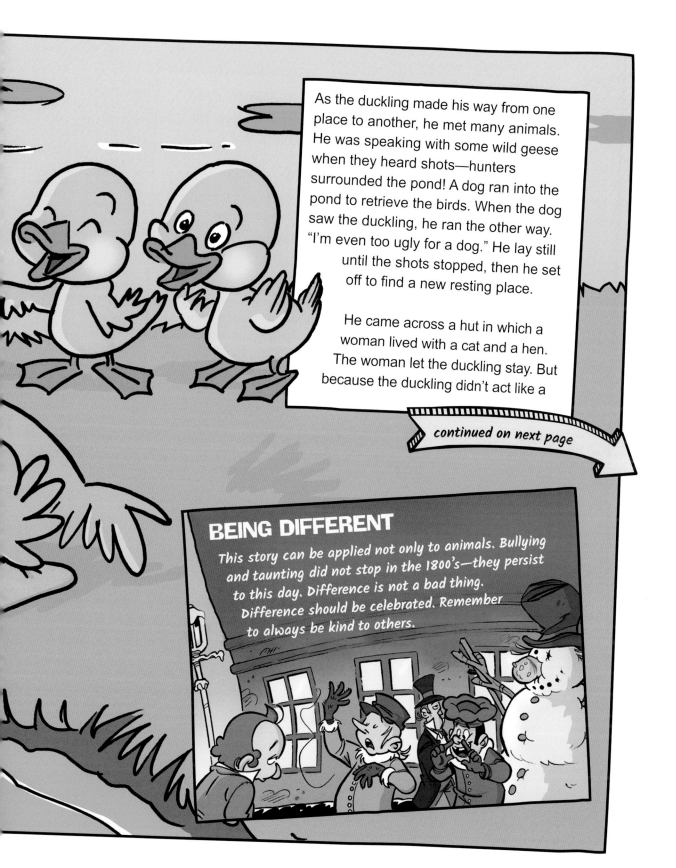

As the duckling made his way from one place to another, he met many animals. He was speaking with some wild geese when they heard shots—hunters surrounded the pond! A dog ran into the pond to retrieve the birds. When the dog saw the duckling, he ran the other way. "I'm even too ugly for a dog." He lay still until the shots stopped, then he set off to find a new resting place.

He came across a hut in which a woman lived with a cat and a hen. The woman let the duckling stay. But because the duckling didn't act like a

continued on next page

BEING DIFFERENT

This story can be applied not only to animals. Bullying and taunting did not stop in the 1800's—they persist to this day. Difference is not a bad thing. Difference should be celebrated. Remember to always be kind to others.

cat and couldn't lay eggs like a hen, the duckling was useless to the household. Soon, the duckling missed the fresh air. He missed floating in water. So he went in search of a pond.

Seasons changed. Animals ignored the duckling. One evening, the duckling saw the most wonderful sight he had ever seen. He saw a flock of beautiful birds. Their white feathers glistened. They had long, graceful necks. The duckling looked at them as they flew off into the distance.

As winter came, the duckling tried to prevent some water from freezing. But the ice closed around him. He froze until a farmer saw him and brought him home. The family tried to play with him, but the duckling thought they were trying to hurt them. He flew out of the house and hid in nearby bushes.

MY LIFE'S STORY

When I write my fairy tales, I like to draw from my own experiences. There is no better example of that than "The Ugly Duckling." I was always a bit self-conscious about my large size—particularly the size of my nose. Despite my many talents, I thought people were poking fun of my Pinocchio-style nose. This fairy tale is the story of my life.

When spring came, the duckling spread its wings. "Spring is here!" His strong wings took him far. He flew above a beautiful garden. Suddenly, he spotted the beautiful birds he had seen before. He was scared that the birds wouldn't accept him, but he decided to swim over anyway. As the beautiful birds approached him, he hung his head in disgust. "Surely they won't like me." He looked at his reflection. He was beautiful! He was a swan!

Everyone said he was the most beautiful swan of them all. But he never became too proud. He soaked up the sunshine and observed his new home. He had never dreamed of such happiness.

THE MAN BEHIND THE INK

The illustrator Thierry Capezzone brought my character to life. He is a French comic book artist now living in Denmark. I would have loved to know him while I was writing my fairy tales. I'm sure we would have inspired each other. Thierry knows so much about me, but I do not know much about him. So, my fellow ghosts and I turn our attention to Thierry. It is time for a little Q&A (that's question and answer).

Thierry Capezzone

Q: What sparks imagination?

A: Many things! Imagination comes from things we see every day. Imagination can also come from a book or just a scene in a street. Everything can spark your imagination if you are curious about life and open to others.

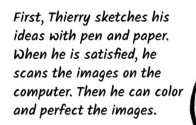

First, Thierry sketches his ideas with pen and paper. When he is satisfied, he scans the images on the computer. Then he can color and perfect the images.

Q: Why do you love drawing comic books?

A: When I was around 9 years old, my mother owned a small grocery store in Lyon, France. One day, I came home from school and an old lady needed help carrying her groceries to her fifth-floor apartment. And there wasn't an elevator! I helped her carry the groceries and, to thank me, the woman opened a huge closet filled with comic books. I think my love of comic books comes from there.

Q: Any tips for young artists?

A: Don't do it like the others. Try to find what suits you best. Experiment until you feel nice and cozy with what you use.

Created and illustrated by
Thierry Capezzone

Written by
Jan Rybka

Directed by Tom Evans
Designed by Brenda Tropinski
Illustration colored by Mike Deporter and Natalia Hansen
The H.C. Chronicles written by Madeline King
Photo edited by Rosalia Bledsoe
Proofread by Nathalie Strassheim
Manufacturing led by Anne Fritzinger

World Book, Inc.
180 North LaSalle Street, Suite 900
Chicago, Illinois 60601
USA

For information about other World Book print and digital publications, please go to
www.worldbook.com or call 1-800-WORLDBK (967-5325).

For information about sales to schools and libraries,
call 1-800-975-3250 (United States) or 1-800-837-5365 (Canada).

Library of Congress Cataloging-in-Publication Data for this volume has been applied for.

The Adventures of Young H.C. Andersen
ISBN: 978-0-7166-0958-2 (set, hc.)

The Adventures of Young H.C. Andersen and the Monk's Secret
ISBN: 978-0-7166-0962-9 (hc.)

Also available as:
ISBN: 978-0-7166-0967-4 (e-book)

Printed in the United States of America
by CG Book Printers, North Mankato, Minnesota
1st printing March 2020

Photo credits: Dutch National Archives: 51 (Joop van Bilsen/Anefo);
© Getty Images: 48 (Grafissimo), 50 (Betty Galella), 55 (Binder/ullstein
bild), (Jack Mitchell); © H.C. Andersen Museum: 56-57; © Yvan Molinaro:
62-63; Public Domain: 51, 54; © RKO Radio Pictures: 50; Royal Danish
Library: 49; © Shutterstock: 48 (Lorelyn Medina), (Aqua),
49 (dinvector), (Everett Historical), 53 (Lexan); © Walt Disney: 55;
WORLD BOOK photos by Don Di Sante: 52, 53.

WORLD
BOOK
www.worldbook.com

Museets rekonstruktion af kugleposten under en karetur i 1936.